Family

Moon

Dad

Mum

my sister, the Witch Baby

Oliver Moon and the Spell-Off

Sue Mongredien

Illustrated by

Jan McCafferty

USBORNE

For Harry Graves, with lots of love

First published in 2007 by Usborne Publishing Ltd., Usborne House, 83-85 Saffron Hill, London EC1N 8RT, England. www.usborne.com

Text copyright © Sue Mongredien Ltd., 2007

Illustration copyright © Usborne Publishing Ltd., 2007

A CIP catalogue record for this book is available from the British Library.

JFMAM JASOND/07   ISBN 9780746077948

Printed in Great Britain.

Contents

Chapter One

The Moon family were sitting down to breakfast one morning when they heard a familiar rattle from the front door. "Post-ghost coming!" the letterbox announced. "Late as usual, I see – what a surprise! Oof!"

There was a thud, as the post fell onto the doormat.

"No need to be so rough!" Oliver heard the letterbox scold the post-ghost. "Just because you're in a hurry! Shouldn't have overslept again, should you?"

Mr. Moon, Oliver's dad, frowned. "That letterbox gets cheekier and cheekier," he commented, with a slurp of his cockroach coffee. "Must get round to putting a magic muffler on it."

The Witch Baby, Oliver's sister, was straining to get out of her high chair. "Down!" she was saying excitedly. "Me see ghost!"

Mrs. Moon gave her a smile. "Not today, pickle," she replied. "He's already gone. Eat up your beetle flakes, there's a good girl."

Oliver finished his batwing toast, and got down from the table to collect the post.

"Not much this morning," the letterbox told him, swinging open as it spoke. "A letter for your dad there, and your mum's *Witch Weekly* magazine. Oh, and some bills, too, I'm afraid." It shut again with a loud snap.

"Thanks," Oliver said politely, gathering up the pile and taking it to his parents. It was a Saturday morning, so there was no rush for him to go to Magic School, or for his dad to fly off to work. He sat back down at the table, and spread some jellyfish jam on a second slice of toast.

"Ooh," his mum said, flicking through her new magazine. "*Green* capes are in this season. Nice… And, ooh, those pumpkin fritters look yummy, I wonder how you—"

She was interrupted by Mr. Moon jumping to his feet with a shout. "I've got it!" he yelled, waving his letter in the air. "I've actually got it!"

"Got what?" Oliver asked with interest.

His dad had jumped up so quickly, he'd knocked the plate of batwing toast off the table.

"Fleas," giggled his sister. "Daddy got fleas!"

Mrs. Moon dragged her eyes away from "101 New Pumpkin Recipes" to look at her husband. "What's that, dear?" she asked distractedly.

"The job!" Mr. Moon cried, a grin on his face. He flung his arms wide, elbowing a vase of stinkweed off the shelf behind him in all the excitement. "I got the job!"

"Really?" Oliver's mum jumped to her feet, fritters forgotten. "Let's see!"

"What job?" Oliver asked. "What are you talking about? You're leaving ValuStix?"

"I certainly am," said Mr. Moon, passing the letter to his wife with a flourish. "I've been offered a job, Oliver. At your school!"

Oliver's eyes boggled at the news. His dad working at Magic School? Oliver knew Mr. Moon had never really enjoyed his job as a broomstick salesman, but he'd had no idea he was thinking of leaving. "But… But…" he stammered, trying to take it in. "But what are you going to be doing at Magic School? You're not… You're not going to be a *teacher*, are you?"

Oliver crossed his fingers behind his back. He really didn't want his dad to be one of his teachers. It would be so embarrassing!

"Not a teacher, no," his dad replied. "I'm the new Potions assistant. I'll be helping out with the experiments, that sort of thing."

"Well done, darling!" Mrs. Moon cried, throwing her arms around her husband's neck. "That's so exciting!"

Oliver stared at his beaming parents. He couldn't help feeling surprised. The current Potions assistant at school, Mr. Newt, was one of the cleverest people Oliver had ever met. Whereas Mr. Moon... Well. He was just...*Dad.*

"Um…Dad," Oliver said, choosing his words carefully, "do you actually *know* much about potions?"

Mr. Moon shrugged. "Well, I *used* to," he said breezily. "Quite a few years ago, anyway. Won the school prize for Potions, back when I was a lad." He smiled. He poured himself another cup of cockroach coffee, splashing some on the tablecloth by mistake.

"And it can't be any harder than trying to flog a load of crummy broomsticks every day! What could possibly go wrong?"

Oliver finished his breakfast thoughtfully. He didn't want to pour cold water on his dad's excitement, but Mr. Newt was always telling them that you needed a steady hand in the Potions room, especially when you were using live ingredients. And Mr. Moon was rather... well, clumsy at times. *And* there was all sorts of new Potions equipment at school that his dad would have to learn to use.

Oliver couldn't help feeling slightly nervous at the thought of his dad working in the Potions room. In his opinion, there were *lots* of things that could go wrong!

Chapter Two

A week or so later, Oliver and Jake were joined on their usual morning walk to school by Mr. Moon. It was his first day in his new job. "Isn't this exciting?" he kept saying. "Isn't this fun? All of us going to school together, eh?"

Oliver looked over at Jake, who was bouncing his skull football in silence.

Usually on a Monday morning, Oliver and Jake chatted non-stop about Saturday's big wizardball match, or what they'd got up to over the weekend. It wasn't really the same with Mr. Moon walking between them.

"Um…yeah, Dad," Oliver replied after a moment. They'd reached the school gates now, and he stopped. "Dad – the staff room is that way. Go and ask for Mrs. MacLizard. She'll sort you out. Good luck and…be careful!"

Oliver watched his dad go, and crossed his fingers. He hoped everything would go all right in the Potions room. He'd been testing his dad on his ingredients last night, and was a bit worried that Mr. Moon seemed to have forgotten almost *everything* about potions. He kept getting frogspawn and toadspawn muddled up, he couldn't tell the cat claws from the bat claws, and he'd knocked over a whole box of red ants by mistake.

"Steady hand, Dad!" Oliver had reminded him, wincing as the Witch Baby tried to eat a handful of wriggling ants.

Oliver crossed the fingers on his other hand too, as he saw his dad walk into the school. Oh, he so hoped Dad would be okay!

Later on, Oliver's class had their Potions lesson as usual. It was strange, walking into the Potions room without cheerful

Mr. Newt greeting everybody by name.
Instead, there was Mr. Moon at the back
of the room. Oliver bit his lip as he saw
that his dad was trying to wrestle a long,
hissing snake back into its glass box. Mr.
Moon already had a strange purple stain
down the front of his overalls, Oliver
noticed in alarm.

"Ahh, our new assistant," Oliver's
teacher, Mr. Goosepimple, said politely.
"Class – this is Mr. Moon. Is...er...is
everything all right there, Mr. Moon?"

The class watched with interest as Mr.
Moon squeezed the squirming snake
safely back into its box and locked the
lid. Then he turned to face the class,
red-faced and panting slightly, but
trying to smile. "Hi, everyone," he said.

In the front row, Lucy Lizardlegs was giggling and nudging her best friend Carly Catstail.

Oliver wondered why — until he noticed the death beetles crawling out of Mr. Moon's front pocket. What were they doing *there*?

"What's that in your dad's ear?" Jake hissed, elbowing Oliver.

Oliver hardly dared look. But when he did… Oh, no. There was a weevilworm coiled around Mr. Moon's ear lobe. Had his dad forgotten that weevilworms gave nasty little nips?

"Right, let's get on with our lesson," Mr. Goosepimple said, with another rather apprehensive glance at Mr. Moon. "We're going to make a Slime potion today. I believe Mr. Moon has already prepared the ingredients for this, so—"

CREEEEAK!

Mr. Goosepimple stopped speaking

as the classroom door opened. Mrs.
MacLizard, the head teacher, walked into
the room, with her arm around a boy
Oliver didn't recognize. The boy looked
to be around Oliver's age, and was
staring around the room with a smirk on
his face.

"Sorry to interrupt," Mrs. MacLizard said, "but I'd like to introduce you all to Casper, my nephew. He's staying with me for a few weeks, so I thought he should join your class for that time. Everybody, this is Casper. He's sure to teach you all a thing or two, he's *very* bright!"

She ruffled Casper's hair fondly, and he stared down his nose at Oliver's classmates.

"Now, Casper, this is the Potions room," Mrs. MacLizard went on. "Casper is an *expert* on Potions, by the way. So what are we making in here, then?"

A sudden yelp came from Mr. Moon's direction. Everyone turned to see him clamping a hand to his ear, trying to wrench off the weevilworm that had sunk its fangs in.

Lucy and Carly tittered again. Some of the boys sniggered. And Bully Bogeywort, Oliver's worst enemy at school, laughed out loud.

"Everything all right, Mr. Moon?" Mrs. MacLizard asked.

"Yes…fine…" grunted Mr. Moon, wincing in pain. The weevilworm finally came away with a tearing sound, and Mr. Moon shook it off his fingers and onto the floor. "Sorry – do carry on. Don't mind me!"

There was a small pause, then Mr. Goosepimple turned back to the head teacher. "We're practising our Slime potions," he told her. "Perhaps you'd like to stay and watch while we put one together? Mr. Moon – if you'd be so kind as to hand round the ingredients?"

Mr. Moon looked rather nervous under the beady eyes of Mrs. MacLizard, Oliver thought. He watched his dad hurry around with the potion ingredients, handing them to each student.

"Thank you, Mr. Moon," said Mr. Goosepimple. "Now, we made this potion last Tuesday, didn't we? So let's see how well you remember it. Pippi, would you demonstrate it for us, please?"

Pippi Prowlcat beamed and got to her feet. Oliver could tell she was proud at the chance to show off her cleverness with the head teacher in the room. "First, I'll put in a spoonful of spider legs," she said loudly, measuring some and tipping them into her potion beaker. "And then a cupful of snake spit…"

She carefully measured out the snake
spit – and Oliver saw his dad turn pale.
"Snake spit?" Mr. Moon muttered, as
Pippi poured it into the beaker. "But
that's not… Oh, no. No! WAIT!" But it
was too late. There was an almighty

BOOM! from the beaker, a scream from Pippi…and then clouds of billowing black smoke engulfed the whole classroom.

Chapter
Three

"Sorry, everybody!" Mr. Moon shouted
through the smoke. "I thought it was
supposed to be *snail slime*!"

Oliver and the rest of the class began
coughing and spluttering in the thick
smoke. Oliver's eyes stung and he tried to
fan it away from his face. He couldn't see
a thing!

"Pippi, are you all right?" Mr. Goosepimple called anxiously. "Pippi?"

Mrs. MacLizard's voice rang out before Pippi could reply. "Vanish, smoke! This is no joke!" she chanted. Oliver heard her wand swishing through the air and then, seconds later, the smoke cleared.

Oliver blinked and rubbed his eyes as the last few black curls of smoke vanished into the end of Mrs. MacLizard's wand. "There," she said, gazing around. "Is everyone okay?"

Pippi Prowlcat had soot all over her face and a singed plait. "What…what happened?" she asked.

"So sorry, all my fault," Mr. Moon said, rushing over to her. "Are you okay? I must have got the snake spit and snail slime muddled up, you see, I…"

Mr. Goosepimple's eyebrows shot up. "That explains it," he said wearily.

"I thought *everyone* knew that putting together spider legs and snail slime causes explosions?" said Bully Bogeywort scornfully, staring at Mr. Moon as if he were a particularly stupid kind of troll.

Oliver glared at him, then at Casper, as the new boy sniggered loudly.

"I'm dreadfully sorry," Mr. Moon said again, wringing his hands. He looked at Pippi. "Your poor hair! Shall I see if I can make you a Hair-conditioning potion, to grow that plait back?"

"No!" squealed Pippi, clapping her hands to her hair and stepping away from Mr. Moon.

"I could do it," drawled Casper, looking highly amused. "But I'd rather choose my own ingredients, thanks all the same."

"I've got some in my office you can use,

dear," Mrs. MacLizard told him, beckoning Pippi over. "Come along, Pippi. Thank you, Mr. Goosepimple. I hope the rest of the lesson is...*quieter* for you."

Casper snorted, then followed his aunt and Pippi out of the room.

Oliver watched them go, then glanced over at his dad, who was gingerly picking up Pippi's blackened beaker.

"Shall we try again?" Mr. Goosepimple said. He didn't sound very pleased, Oliver thought. "Mr. Moon, perhaps you could retrieve all the snail slime and give the students snake spit, as instructed. Then we might be able to get somewhere!"

"Yes, Mr. Goosepimple, of course, Mr. Goosepimple," Oliver's dad said, wiping his sooty hands on his overalls. "Snake spit coming right up. Um...whereabouts is it again?"

"Never mind," Mrs. Moon comforted her husband later that evening. The Witch Baby had just gone to bed, and Oliver and his parents were in the living room. "Everyone makes mistakes on their first day. Remember when I used to work at the Spell Supplies shop in town, and I turned my boss into a dragon's egg, on *my* first day?"

"And Pippi's plait *did* grow back again with the hair restorer...well, kind of," Oliver said, trying to be encouraging. "It's not quite the same colour as the rest of her hair, but..."

Mr. Moon nodded. "I suppose you're right," he said. "I'm sure tomorrow will be better. I just need a bit of practice, that's all. Hadn't realized quite how rusty I'd got."

"Oh, you'll pick it up soon, I'm sure," Mrs. Moon said confidently.

Oliver grimaced as he remembered the look on Mrs. MacLizard's face in the Potions lab that afternoon. He really hoped his dad had a better day at Magic School tomorrow — for everyone's sake. He didn't want Bully *or* Casper to have anything to tease him about!

Chapter
Four

Over the next couple of days, Oliver got to know Casper a little better – and his first impressions weren't good. Casper was a brilliant wizard, but such a show-off with it!

When Casper was casting an Obedience Charm over some woolly spiders, they didn't just stay still to listen, they actually sat down on their back four legs to pay full attention to him. With a smug smile on his face, Casper called the whole class over to watch as he commanded his spiders to balance in a tall, spindly-legged tower.

Oliver, whose own spiders seemed more interested in spinning webs down the table leg, could hardly bear to look.

On the next day, when Casper used the Transforma spell to turn grains of rice into giant headlice, he cast the spell so perfectly that the headlice all lined up neatly on Casper's desk, before leaping one by one into Nina Nettlewick's bunches.

Oliver's giant headlice, on the other hand, were *too* giant. He had to cast a quick Stun spell to stop them before they made a break for anyone's hair and took an ear off with their great jaws.

If the new boy was showing his brilliance, the new Potions assistant was doing just the opposite. Poor Mr. Moon wasn't doing at all well in his new job. On Tuesday, he sent half the Year Fours home with food poisoning, after he spilled a jar of tox-beetles into a Full-belly potion they were making.

And on Wednesday, he got eagle bones

confused with seagull bones when the
Year Twelves were making Flying potions.
Once they'd drunk their potions, the Year
Twelves were transformed into seagulls
and flew miles to the coast to catch fish.

Mrs. MacLizard had to conjure up a special Summoning spell to get them all back to Cacklewick.

"What an idiot he is," Bully Bogeywort had sneered that afternoon. "Mr. Moon? Mr. Buffoon, more like!"

"Watch it!" Oliver had snapped hotly. "That's my dad you're talking about."

Casper had joined in. "So you must be Oliver Buffoon, then," he'd sniggered. "Right?"

"Wrong," Oliver had growled. "And my dad's not a buffoon. He's only just started his job, so give him a chance."

"Maybe I should ask my Aunty Madge to give him a chance," Casper had replied smartly. "A chance to get a new job!"

*

On Thursday afternoon, Mr. Moon got slightly muddled up when making a potion for the Year Ten Predictions lesson. Mr. Swish, the teacher, had asked for a "See" potion to help his class see into the future. Unfortunately, Mr. Moon had misunderstood, and had put together a "Sea" potion…which caused a flood of seawater to rush through the building.

It took Mrs. MacLizard half an hour to dry the floors with a Hot-air spell.

Of course, as Oliver and his classmates were outside, playing Wizardball, they got to see the torrents of water that came pouring out of the school. And it didn't take them long to find out who had caused it. Bully Bogeywort laughed so hard, he almost fell over.

"He's a disaster, that man. A total disaster!" Bully Bogeywort guffawed. "A zombie would do a better job!"

"Shut up, Bogey-brain," Oliver snapped. "Leave him alone. Everyone makes mistakes."

Bully Bogeywort fixed Oliver with his mean yellow eyes. "That's true, Oliver. And I'm looking at his *biggest* mistake right now – you."

"Oh, go away," Oliver said. "Go and fall off your broomstick somewhere painful."

"Ignore him, Ol," Jake said, bouncing his ball. "He's just jealous, because he knows you're the best wizard in the class. Come on, let's practise a few hoops."

"What? Oliver Buffoon, the best wizard in the class?" Bully Bogeywort replied, his eyes flicking across the wizardball court to where Casper was shooting perfect practice goals one after another. "No chance. Not while Casper's here."

"Oliver's just as good a wizard as Casper is!" Jake retorted.

"Oh yeah?" Bully Bogeywort sneered, stalking away. "We'll see."

Oliver and Jake began passing the ball back and forth, taking turns to throw it through the Wizardball ring.

When everyone had warmed up, Ms. Smokeweaver, the Wizardball coach, split them into teams for a match. Casper was captain of the purple team, and Oliver was captain of the yellow team. Just as Ms Smokeweaver blew her whistle to end the match, Casper scored the winning goal. "Well done, Purples – ten-nine, an amazing victory!" she cried. "Now off you go to get changed, everyone, it's home time."

Oliver felt crushed as he and Jake put on their school cloaks and set off for home. He was sick of Casper being so good at everything all the time. Just as he was about to say as much to Jake, a messenger sprite appeared in a thick cloud of green smoke.

"Message!" the sprite trilled. "Oliver Moon – your dad's a loser, and so are you. I challenge you to a spell-off. Four spells and a potion tomorrow after school. From Casper!"

"What?" Oliver asked, blinking as the smoke swirled around his face. "A loser? A spell-off?"

"That's what I just said," the sprite replied, bowing deeply. "Magic competition, innit? Best wizard wins. Laters!"

The sprite vanished without another word. "Of all the cheek!" Oliver muttered crossly. "Who does that Casper think he is?"

"He's not messing about, is he?" Jake replied. "Four spells and a potion. Blimey. Serious stuff."

"Here he comes now," Oliver said, as they headed down towards the school drive. Students were pouring down it, some on broomsticks, some walking –

and there was Casper striding up behind
Oliver and Jake. His cape swished along
behind him, like big black wings. As
Casper came nearer, Oliver saw that the
new boy's eyes looked cold and hard.

"So, you think you're better than me, do you?" Casper said fiercely. "Think you can beat me in a spell-off?"

Oliver stared at him in disbelief. What a nerve he had, coming to Magic School and picking fights like that! Why did he have it in for Oliver, anyway?

A hot feeling of rage surged through him. Well, he'd show Casper! "Yeah," he replied. "I do. And if I win, then you've got to promise never to say another mean word about me or my dad, okay?"

Casper laughed. "No problem," he replied confidently. He folded his arms in front of him. "And if *I* win – *when* I win, rather – you've got to shut up about my Aunty Madge."

"What?" Oliver asked, feeling

bewildered. What had Mrs. MacLizard got to do with anything? "I never—"

Casper hadn't finished. "And to make it more interesting, let's throw in a little forfeit for the loser, too," he added, glaring.

"Fine," Oliver snapped. Then he wondered what he was letting himself in for. But he couldn't back down now! "What sort of a forfeit?" he asked.

Casper thought for a moment. "Whoever loses the spell-off," he said slowly, "has to fly up to the highest school tower, and ride their broomstick right round it… blindfolded!"

Oliver gulped as he stared up at the tallest school tower. It was very, very high indeed. In fact, on a cloudy day, you couldn't even see the top of it!

"I don't think that's such a good idea," Jake said.

Casper leaned forward, a scornful look on his face. "Not…scared, are you, Oliver?" he asked.

Oliver shook his head. "No way," he fibbed. He held out his hand. "It's a deal," he said. "After school tomorrow."

Casper grabbed Oliver's hand and shook it hard, squeezing Oliver's fingers together. "Looking forward to it," he said.

Chapter Five

"I'll show him," Oliver said through gritted teeth as Casper marched away, nose in the air.

"Will you?" Jake asked doubtfully.

Oliver's shoulders slumped, and he couldn't help a little sigh. "Well…I hope so," he said. He stared after the new boy as he stalked off into the distance. "What did Casper mean, do you think, when he said he wanted me to shut up about Mrs. MacLizard?"

Jake shook his head. "No idea. What have you been saying about her?"

"Nothing!" Oliver protested. "I can't *think* of anything I might have said, anyway." He couldn't help staring up at the top tower again. It looked even higher than it had done two minutes ago. He really, *really* didn't want to fly all the way up there on his broomstick. He *had* to beat Casper in the spell-off. He just had to!

That night, Oliver got down to some serious swotting. Four spells and a potion, the messenger sprite had said. That meant he and Casper would be choosing two spells each to challenge one another with. So Oliver had to come up with two difficult ones, which he'd be able to do but hopefully Casper couldn't, as well as prepare for whatever the new boy might throw at him. Knowing Casper, he'd probably pick some really obscure ones that Oliver had never even heard of.

Oliver worked hard all evening, until the Midnight Moon shone through his bedroom window, and his mum came and told him to turn the lamp off and go to bed. He fell asleep whispering spells to himself, and crossing all of his fingers.

When Oliver walked into the classroom the next morning at school, Casper was poring over a heavy spell book, nodding to himself in a pleased manner. He looked up and saw Oliver, then tapped a finger on the page he'd been reading and smirked. "This is going to sort the wizard from the wannabe," he said loudly. "You just wait, Oliver Moon."

Oliver sat down, feeling tense. Bully

Bogeywort caught his eye and winked. "I've been hearing all about this little spell-off. Can I watch?" he asked loudly.

"No way," Oliver said. It was bad enough doing the spell-off in the first place, but it would be even worse with Bully Bogeywort hanging around making stupid comments.

"We *do* need a judge," Casper put in, overhearing.

"Yeah, but not *him*," Oliver said.

"I'll do it," Jake offered.

Casper narrowed his eyes. "But you're Oliver's friend! A judge isn't supposed to take sides," he pointed out.

"I won't!" Jake protested. "I'll—"

But Casper was already asking Colin Cockroach if he'd do it. "Sure," Colin said. "Loser flies round the tall tower, did you say? This I've got to see!"

Oliver felt sick all day. He could hardly concentrate in Cauldron Cookery. He couldn't sit still in Sorcery. And he fidgeted all the way through Fairy

Physics. After school had finished, Oliver, Jake, Casper and Colin walked along to the Potions room. Oliver's heart was pounding. His hands felt clammy. He really, really wished he could go home like everyone else right now.

Once in the Potions room, Colin fished in his cloak pocket for a coin, flipped it up into the air and slapped it down on his hand. "Oliver – hat or broomstick?"

"Hat," Oliver replied.

Colin uncovered the coin and they all bent over it. A broomstick was clearly visible on the silver coin. "Casper goes first," he declared solemnly.

Casper and Oliver walked to opposite ends of the room. Casper gave Oliver another of his frosty looks. "The first spell is...to conjure up a sky-dragon!" he called out.

Oliver's mind went blank. A sky-dragon? Oh, no! That was a really hard spell. He racked his brains, then waved his wand, chanting the words of the spell as they came to him. *"Lizard's leg and beetle's eye,"* he began hesitantly – then smiled in relief as he suddenly remembered the rest. *"I call a dragon to the sky!"*

There was a shower of silver sparks
from his wand, and then a red dragon
appeared in front of Oliver. It hovered in
mid-air, flicking its scaly tail.

On the other side of the room, Casper's
spell seemed to have worked perfectly too,

as a huge golden dragon had appeared.
It charged at the red dragon and
breathed fire on it. With a screech of fear,
the red dragon disappeared.

"One-nil to Casper," Colin said,
backing away.

Casper smiled and clapped his hands. The golden dragon turned into thousands of tiny golden sparkles, then vanished completely.

Oliver gripped his wand, his mouth dry. Now it was his turn. He really hoped Casper would struggle with *this* one. "The second spell is to…turn yourself invisible!" he shouted.

He waved his wand, and chanted the spell: "*Make me not there, turn me to…*"

Oliver started coughing. His mouth was so dry, he could hardly get the last word out. "*Air!*" he croaked hoarsely.

Across the other side of the room, he could see that Casper had completely disappeared. Rats!

He looked down at himself. His left

foot was still clearly visible for all to see. Double rats!

"Sorry, Ol," Jake said. "I can still see you."

"It's two-nil to Casper!" Colin announced.

Casper appeared again, grinning. "I'm enjoying this," he said. "Spell number three. Oh, and if I beat you on this one, then I've won, right? Better get that blindfold ready, Oliver!"

Oliver wiped his sweaty hands on his cloak. "Get on with it," he muttered.

"Spell number three," Casper said. "Make yourself fly!"

Oliver thought back to his dad's eagle/seagull disaster as he raised his wand, ready to wave it. But before he could open his mouth, Casper had already chanted a spell and he rose off the ground triumphantly, flapping his arms and sticking out his tongue.

A brilliant idea struck Oliver then, and he waved his wand over himself. Everyone knew that eagles could fly higher than wizards, didn't they? Maybe if he went one better than a simple flying command, he could beat Casper this time!

"Wing and claw and beady eye.

Let me fly like eagles fly!" he shouted.

Instantly, feathers began sprouting all over his body, and his arms became wings. Oliver laughed out loud as he flapped them hard and soared effortlessly off the ground, leaving Casper far below.

Jake let out a cheer. "Surely Oliver wins that one?"

Colin nodded. "Oliver pulls one back. It's two-one to Casper!"

Casper scowled. "When I said flying, I meant as a wizard," he said, landing on the ground once more with a thump.

Oliver did a loop the loop over the ingredients cupboard. "Can't hear you, sorry," he called. "I'm too high up!"

Once Oliver had landed and turned back into his usual self, he took a deep breath. His turn now, and the next spell he'd chosen was a difficult one. If Casper muddled it up, Oliver could even the score up to two-all. "Spell number four — become a lion!" he shouted.

He waved his wand for a fourth time, chanting the spell as he did so.

"Mane and tail,
Growl and claw,
This lion has a powerful ROAR!"

He felt his body expanding, and then fur began sprouting all over him. He dropped down on all fours, swishing his tail and growling.

The same thing happened to Casper, and within moments there were two lions

baring their teeth at each other across
the lab.

Colin stepped between them and eyed
them cautiously. "No fighting, no biting,
judge's rules," he said, with a nervous
catch in his voice. He looked from one

lion to the other. "Hmmm. Both excellent. Too close to call," he decided. "This one's a draw! Score stays at two-one to Casper."

Oliver roared in disappointment as he turned back into a boy once more. He'd really thought he was going to get that point, too! Which meant that as the score stood, he just *had* to win the last round. Otherwise…

Oliver gulped. Otherwise Casper would have won the spell-off and he, Oliver, would be flying around the top tower, blindfolded!

Chapter Six

"The final round is the Potions test,"
Colin said. "To make things fair, I'm
going to flick through the Potions book
and open it at random, okay?"

Casper and Oliver both nodded, and
Colin shut his eyes and ran a thumb
down the pages of the big black Potions
book that lived in the lab. "This one!"

he declared, opening it halfway through.

The Potions book gave a chuckle. "He's picked a good 'un!" it said in a breathy, rustling sort of a voice. "The Hooting potion! Get it right, and you'll hoot like an owl. Get it wrong, and you'll squawk like a parrot."

Oliver couldn't help a nervous flinch. He'd never tried the Hooting potion before. He scanned the ingredients list quickly, as did Casper. A dozen hairy caterpillars, three feathers from an owl, a slither of toadspawn...

"Collect your ingredients...now!" Jake called.

Oliver and Casper rushed down to the

Potions cupboard, and grabbed a beaker
each. With trembling fingers, Oliver
counted out twelve hairy caterpillars,
and then three white owl feathers.
Casper did the same.

And then, just as they reached for the toadspawn jar, Oliver saw a label on it, in his dad's handwriting. The frogspawn jar also had a label with Mr. Moon's loopy handwriting. And Oliver hesitated. He knew very well that his dad always, *always* got frogspawn and toadspawn muddled up. That meant the jar that read "toadspawn" would really have frogspawn in it. And the jar labelled "frogspawn" was sure to have toadspawn in it.

Casper opened the jar marked "toadspawn" and scooped some out into his jar. "That's me done," he announced, pushing past Oliver to get to his desk.

While Casper started on his potion, Oliver took the jar marked "frogspawn"

and spooned out a dollop. It was a
gamble, he knew. But he had to give it
a go.

The two boys worked in silence,
grinding and heating and mixing, until
they both had a potion ready. Casper's
was bright green. Oliver's was yellow.

"Interesting," Casper said, raising his eyebrows. "After three? One, two, three… DRINK!"

Both boys lifted their beakers to their mouths and then, crossing his fingers with his free hand, Oliver took a big mouthful and swallowed it down.

Ugh! It tasted absolutely vile. "Too-whit-too-whoo!" he hooted in disgust. And then his mouth fell open in delight. He'd hooted! He'd got it right! And it was all thanks to his dad, getting it *wrong*!

Casper let out a squawk…and his face fell. His Hooting potion hadn't worked. He sounded like a parrot.

"Oliver gets a point, so you both finish up with two points each!" Colin announced, and laughed. "It's a draw! So that means Casper, you can't be mean about Oliver's dad any more, and Oliver…" He hesitated. "What was your side of the deal, Casper?"

The potions were wearing off. Casper squawked a few times and then replied. "Oliver can't say anything else horrible about my Aunty Madge," he said firmly.

"Too-whit-too-*what*?" Oliver asked. "I never said anything horrible about her in the first place! I *like* Mrs. MacLizard!"

Casper looked at him suspiciously. "What about that magic message you sent me, then? Where you said I was an egghead and my aunt was a warty walrus?"

"A warty walrus?" echoed Oliver in shock. "I didn't say that! And I didn't call you an egghead either!" He stared at Casper. "You were the one who started the name-calling. What was it you said? That my dad was a loser, and so was I!"

Casper shook his head slowly. "I didn't say any of that," he told Oliver. He narrowed his eyes, thinking. "And I didn't challenge you to this spell-off either."

Oliver gulped. "You didn't? Well, it wasn't *my* idea. So who…?"

The thought struck them at exactly the same time. "Bully Bogeywort," Oliver groaned.

"He set us up!" Casper exclaimed. "The messages were both from him!"

"The double-crossing toad!" Colin gasped.

"Of all the sneaky…" Jake spluttered, shaking his head.

Casper looked thoughtful. "There must be a way we can pay him back," he said. "We can't let him get away with this, Oliver!"

Oliver nodded. "You're right," he said. "Let me think…"

The boys left the Potions room and started walking down the corridor. "We could put a Hairless hex on him," Casper said with a grin. "He'll be bald as a beetle by breakfast."

Oliver spluttered with laughter. "Or we could put a Tight-hat curse on him, so that his pointy hat sticks to his head all day and night," he suggested.

"Hey, look, there he is," Jake said, pointing as Bully Bogeywort stomped out of the main school doors, his broomstick under his arm. "How come he's leaving school so late today?"

"Detention with Mrs. MacLizard for getting caught bunking off Broomstick Training," Colin told them.

They followed Bully out and watched as he swung a leg over his broomstick and prepared to fly off home.

Oliver's eyes gleamed, and he turned to Casper. "I've just had an idea," he said. "Maybe as neither of *us* got to fly around the tallest tower, we should let Bully have the pleasure…"

"Yes!" Casper laughed. "Perfect, Oliver!" He raised his wand with a grin. "You do a Blindfolding spell, and I'll hex his broomstick. Ready…steady…GO!"

The two boys pointed their wands at

Bully Bogeywort and muttered a series of magic words each. Then they all watched as a large pink blindfold appeared from out of nowhere on Bully's face, covering his eyes. In the same moment, his broomstick started jiggling impatiently beneath him.

"Hey!" they heard him cry, trying to rip off the blindfold. "What's this? What's going on?"

"Hold on tight and enjoy the ride, Bully!" Casper shouted out.

"Have fun!" bellowed Oliver.

Then they all stood and watched the extraordinary sight of Bully Bogeywort's broomstick dragging him round and round the tallest tower of the school, while its rider shouted and squealed in fright.

Oliver couldn't stop laughing –
especially when Bully Bogeywort landed
in a huge muddy puddle.

"Priceless," Oliver said, wiping the
tears from his eyes as he watched Bully
wrench off the pink blindfold and look
around in a daze.

Casper turned to Oliver. "I reckon that
was almost worth having to do the spell-
off for!" he said.

Oliver grinned. "Definitely," he said.
"We make a good team! All four of us."

Oliver high-fived his friends, and they
headed home for tea.

The End

Join Oliver and his friends
for more magical mayhem at

www.olivermoon.co.uk

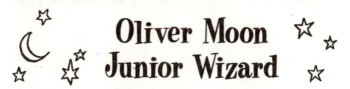

Oliver Moon
Junior Wizard

Collect all of Oliver Moon's magical adventures!

Oliver Moon and the Potion Commotion   ISBN 9780746073063
Trouble is brewing when Oliver Moon is up against his arch-rival in the Young Wizard of the Year award.

Oliver Moon and the Dragon Disaster   ISBN 9780746073070
Oliver is sure he can heat things up a bit at the Festival of Magic with the help of his sister's new pet dragon.

Oliver Moon and the Nipperbat Nightmare ISBN 9780746077917
It's Oliver's turn to look after the school pet, Nippy, for the holidays. But when Nippy escapes things go horribly wrong...

Oliver Moon's Summer Howliday   ISBN 9780746077924
Oliver's summer holiday is going swimmingly until he starts to suspect there is something odd about his hairy new friend, Wilf.

Oliver Moon's Christmas Cracker   ISBN 9780746077931
Oliver is sure Christmas at his horrible Aunt Wart's is going to be dreadful, but can a very special Christmas present save the day?

Oliver Moon and the Spell-off   ISBN 9780746077948
Oliver hopes that he'll win the spell-off against clever Casper, because he can't face the scary forfeit...

And coming soon...

Oliver Moon's Fangtastic Sleepover   ISBN 9780746084793
Oliver is on a school sleepover at a haunted house museum, but will he make it through the night when a swarm of vampire bats arrives?

Oliver Moon and the Broomstick Olympics ISBN 9780746084809
Oliver is excited about entering the Junior Wizards' Obstacle Race, but can he overcome Bully Bogeywort's cheating tactics?

All books are priced at £3.99